Frogs in Clogs

by
Sheila
White
Samton

Crown Publishers, Inc.
New York

For Pat Stiles

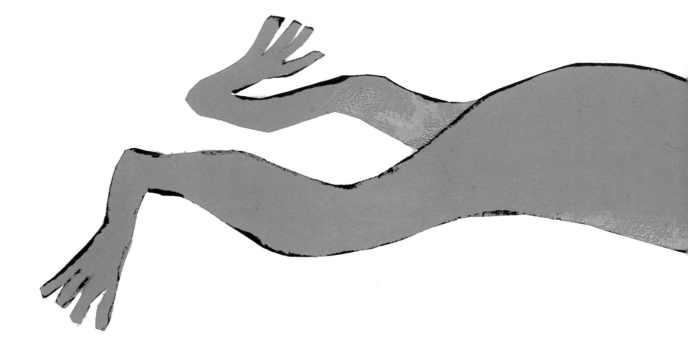

Published by Crown Publishers, Inc.,
a Random House company, 201 East 50th Street,
New York, NY 10022

CROWN is a trademark of Crown Publishers, Inc.

Manufactured in Singapore

Library of Congress Cataloging-in-Publication Data
Samton, Sheila White.
Frogs in clogs / written and illustrated by Sheila White Samton. — 1st ed.
p.   cm.
Summary: Frogs in clogs befriend pigs in wigs and together
they outwit the greedy bugs on rugs.
[1. Animals—Fiction. 2. Stories in rhyme.] I. Title.
PZ8.3.S213Fr   1995
[E]—dc20   94-16391

ISBN 0-517-59874-4 (trade)
0-517-59875-2 (lib. bdg.)

10 9 8 7 6 5 4 3 2

*The illustrations in this book are collages of
acrylic paint on rice paper.
The text is set in Leawood Book 30 pt.*

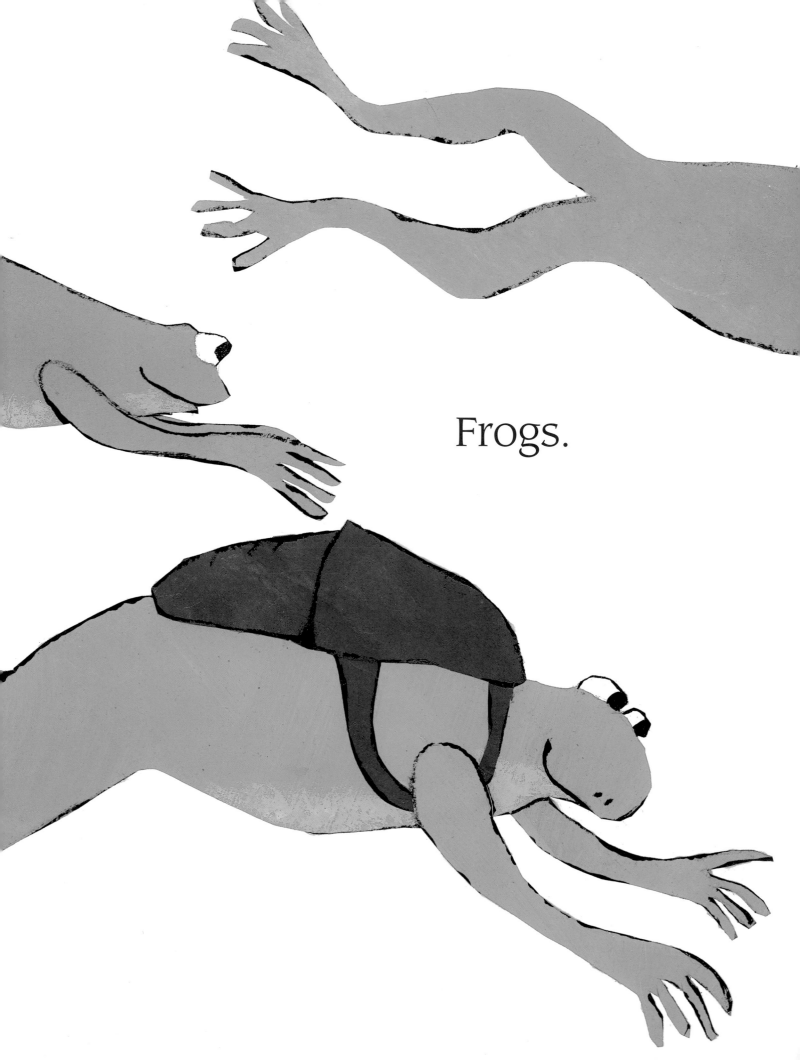

Frogs.

Bog.

Frogs in the bog.

Boggy frogs.
Soggy frogs.

Frogs in clogs!

Pigs.

Figs.

Pigs in the figs.

Piggy pigs. Figgy pigs.

Pigs in wigs!

Pigs in wigs jig into the bog.

Frogs joggle pigs!
Pigs jiggle frogs!

Would you like to share our figs?

Would you like to wear our clogs?

Frogs and pigs
wiggle-woggle
in the bog!

Bugs on rugs,
wearing goggles
in a fog!

Would you like to share our figs?

Bugs want *all* the figs, clogs, wigs!

BIG STRUGGLE IN THE BOG!

Bugs lug pigs to rugs in fog!

Fig on a log?
Fig on a wig?

Follow the figs!
Find our pigs!

Good-bye, bugs.
Big frog hugs!